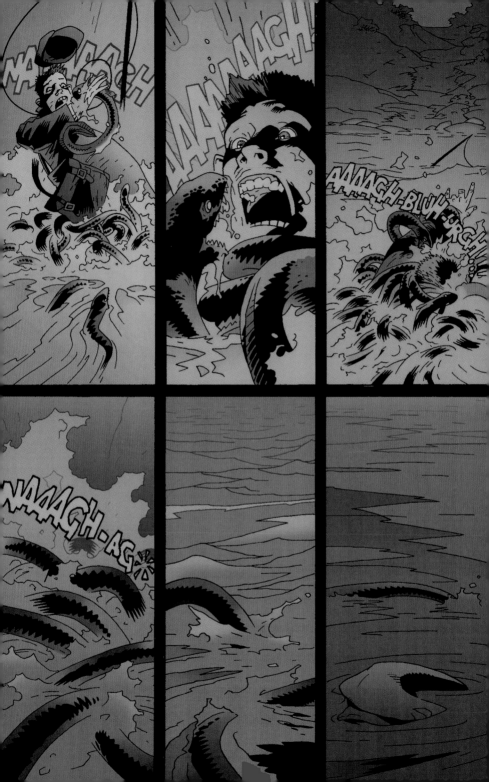

SILVERFIN

THE GRAPHIC NOVEL

CHARLIE HIGSON

&

KEV WALKER

Disney · HYPERION BOOKS

NEW YORK

PART ONE

ETON

WHERE DO I SLEEP?

YOUR BED'S BEHIND HERE.

WE'LL GET YOU SOME MORE FURNITURE. YOU'LL NEED IT.

AFTER ALL, YOU'LL SPEND HALF YOUR LIFE IN THIS ROOM.

Half my life...?

WAKEY, WAKEY. RISE AN' SHINE, YOU LAZY LUMP.

SPLASH!

WHA....!

TIME TO GET UP, MISTER BOND.

OH...YES... RIGHT.

MY NAME'S JAMES BOND.

IT'S MY FIRST TERM...

IT'S CALLED A "HALF," NOT A TERM, YOU LITTLE BRAT.

DON'T YOU WORRY, BOND...

"...I'LL DEAL WITH YOU LATER."

LATIN'S NOT YOUR STRONG POINT, IS IT, JAMES?

EVER THOUGHT ABOUT ATHLETICS?

THIS PLACE IS TAKING SOME GETTING USED TO.

IT'S NOT LIKE I COME FROM AN **ETON** FAMILY.

YOU DON'T TALK ABOUT YOUR FAMILY MUCH, DO YOU?

NO.

I'LL BET THEY'RE CRIMINALS, AREN'T THEY? IN PRISON SOMEWHERE?

OR SPIES WORKING UNDERCOVER.

SORRY TO DISAPPOINT YOU. I'M NOTHING SPECIAL...

BOY?!!

IT'S OK, I'LL GO. I DON'T MIND.

YOU, BOY. ARE YOU MEANT TO BE HERE?

I'M RUNNING AN ERRAND FOR THE CAPTAIN OF THE HOUSE, SIR.

AND WHAT IS YOUR NAME, BOY?

BOND, SIR. JAMES BOND.

BOND?

I USED TO KNOW AN ANDREW BOND. ANY RELATION?

YES, SIR. MY FATHER, SIR.

IT'S A SMALL WORLD. YOUR FATHER AND I ARE IN THE SAME LINE OF BUSINESS.

THE ARMS TRADE?

THAT'S RIGHT. YOUR FATHER STILL WITH VICKERS?

NO, SIR. HE'S...HE'S NOT.

A GOOD MAN, I LIKED HIM. I'M LORD HELLEBORE...

...MAYBE YOU KNOW MY SON, GEORGE.

WE'VE MET.

I WONDER, ARE YOU LIKE HIM? CAN YOU RUN? CAN YOU SWIM? WRESTLE ALLIGATORS?

DO YOU BOX, MISTER BOND?

A LITTLE.

COME ON THEN, SHOW ME.

GO ON, TAKE A SWING AT ME.

THAT THE BEST YOU GOT?

DAD, DO YOU HAVE TO...?

SMAKK

HEY....!

YOU CAUGHT ME OFF GUARD.

COME ALONG, RANDOLPH. WE DON'T WANT TO BE LATE FOR SUPPER.

SURE.

I NEED TO LOOK OUT FOR YOU, MISTER BOND.

EXCELLENT, BOND.

YOU'VE REALLY BUILT UP YOUR STAMINA.

I DON'T THINK THERE ARE MANY WHO COULD BETTER YOU OVER A LONG COURSE NOW.

THANK YOU — phuh — SIR...

THERE'S A BIG EVENT COMING UP AT THE END OF THE HALF. A NEW TROPHY.

THREE GAMES IN ONE DAY...RUNNING, SHOOTING AND SWIMMING.

SWIMMING, SIR? BUT IT'S NOT SUMMER.

I KNOW, BOND. YOU'D HAVE TO BE MAD TO GO IN FOR IT.

ARE YOU MAD?

I'LL GIVE IT A GO.

GOOD MAN. MAYBE THE HELLEBORE CUP WILL BE YOURS.

HELLEBORE?

YOU KNOW THE AMERICAN LAD? IT'S HIS FATHER'S IDEA.

BEEN VERY GENEROUS TO THE SCHOOL, BUT I'M NOT SURE I APPROVE.

MADE ALL HIS MONEY IN THE WAR...SELLING WEAPONS.

TOO MANY BOYS AND MASTERS FROM THE SCHOOL WERE KILLED IN THE WAR.

YOUNG MEN WHO SHOULD HAVE BECOME SCIENTISTS, ARTISTS, AND SPORTSMEN...

...GONE FOREVER.

WHO'S THAT?

OH, IT'S JUST CROAKER. HE LOOKS AFTER THE BOATS. HE'S A BIT MAD.

HELLO, CROAKER. WHAT ARE YOU FISHING FOR?

TAKE A LOOK.

EELS.

THEY CAN'T LET GO OF THE WOOL, SEE? I WOVE WORMS INTO IT.

YOU'RE NOT GOING TO EAT THEM?

COURSE I AM. THEY STEWS UP LOVELY. NICE AND SWEET IS EEL MEAT.

SO... DO YOU STILL WANT TO GO IN FOR THE CUP?

WHY NOT?

I'LL START PRACTICING TOMORROW.

IF YOU'RE NOT PREPARED TO FIGHT, YOU DIE.

YOU HAVE TO DO WHATEVER IT TAKES TO WIN.

OR BE BURIED UNDER THE EXCREMENT OF LESSER MEN!!

SO LET THE GAMES BEGIN!

FIRST, THE SHOOTING...

BOND...

NOT BAD, BOND. VERY RESPECTABLE.

CHEER UP, YOU'RE STILL IN WITH A CHANCE!

THERE'S THE CROSS-COUNTRY TO COME...

"...AND BEFORE THAT THE SWIMMING."

"RIGHT, JAMES, CARLTON'S A STRONG RUNNER, BUT HELLEBORE IS FASTER..."

...IT'S UP TO YOU TO STOP HIM WINNING.

ON YOUR MARKS, GET SET...

CRAKK

HE TOOK A SHORTCUT! I KNEW IT!

CHEAT!

YOU DID IT, YOU DID IT!

WELL DONE, MY BOY. I KNEW YOU COULD DO IT.

WHO... WHO CAME SECOND?

CARLTON'S JUST COME IN NOW.

HE'S WON THE CUP.

PART TWO

SCOTLAND

Dearest James,

I am still up here in Scotland looking after my brother. Yes, I'm afraid that your poor Uncle Max is not getting any better and I do not feel that I can leave him just at the moment. I therefore think that it would be for the best if you made the journey up to Scotland and spent your Easter holidays with us here in Keithly. I am sure that it would do your uncle a power of good to have a young person about the place, and I must confess that I have missed you terribly. I am enclosing your ticket and some extra money for food. I can't tell you how much I am looking forward to seeing you again.

Your loving aunt,

Charmian

TICKETS, PLEASE.

'ERE...COULDN'T DO US A FAVOR, COULD YOU, MATE...?

LOST ME TICKET. BUT I NEED TO GET ON THAT TRAIN.

I'LL SEE WHAT I CAN DO.

TICKET, SON?

ER...I HAVE IT HERE...

...SOMEWHERE...

HURRY UP, MAN, PUT YOUR BACK INTO IT.

The Return of BULLDOG DRUMMOND

ALL ABOAAAARD!

THERE YOU ARE...

YOU!

I WANT TO COME WITH YOU, MOTHER.

WHEN YOU'RE OLDER, JAMES. MOUNTAINEERING'S TOO DANGEROUS.

YOUR AUNT CHARMIAN WILL LOOK AFTER YOU.

GOOD-BYE...

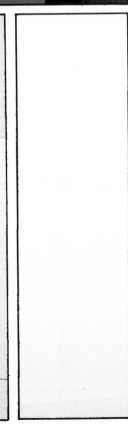

JAMES...

...IT'S YOUR MOTHER AND FATHER. THEY...

THERE'S BEEN AN ACCIDENT.

THEY WON'T BE COMING HOME.

WHAT DO YOU MEAN?

IT NEVER GOES ACCORDING TO PLAN.

I GET TIRED SO EASILY THESE DAYS.

THAT'S OK, UNCLE, I...

I MAY AS WELL ENJOY IT WHILE I CAN— *koff* —

I DON'T THINK I WILL EVER SMOKE.

GOOD FOR YOU. I STARTED DURING THE WAR, I'M AFRAID.

DEATH WAS THE ONLY THING WE COULD BE SURE OF.

YOU NEVER TALK ABOUT THE WAR.

NOT ALLOWED... BUT WHAT HARM CAN IT DO TO TELL YOU NOW?

I WAS A SPY.

WHAT'S THIS I HEAR ABOUT A MISSING BOY?

ALFIE KELLY. POOR LAD. THEY'VE BEEN DRAGGING THE RIVER.

HE WAS A FISHERMAN. THE RIVER WOULDN'T BE A PROBLEM. NOW THE LOCH...

EXACTLY. A CHALLENGE FOR THE LAD. USED TO BE THE BEST FISHING AROUND...

TOSH... THERE'S NO FISHING ALLOWED ON LOCH SILVERFIN.

TILL THAT YANK, HELLEBORE, TOOK OVER AS LAIRD.

LORD HELLEBORE?

THAT'S RIGHT. HIS SON'S AT ETON, TOO, I BELIEVE.

IS HE A FRIEND OF YOURS?

NO.

WAIT!

SHLURL

PLOOSH

WHAT THE HELL...?

CAN I SEE?

SAY, NOW...

...LOOKS LIKE I'VE CAUGHT MYSELF A COUPLA SPIES.

PART THREE

SILVERFIN

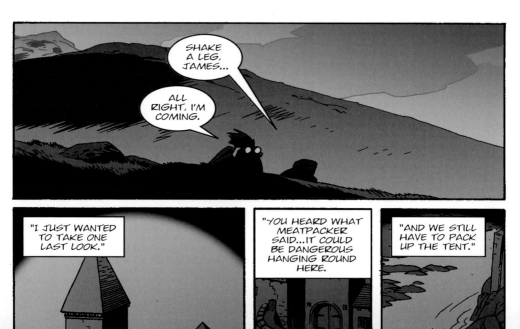

SHAKE A LEG, JAMES...

ALL RIGHT, I'M COMING.

"I JUST WANTED TO TAKE ONE LAST LOOK."

"YOU HEARD WHAT MEATPACKER SAID...IT COULD BE DANGEROUS HANGING ROUND HERE.

"AND WE STILL HAVE TO PACK UP THE TENT."

DON'T YOU EVER STOP MOANING —

WAIT A MINUTE...

EVENIN'.

HE'S AWAKE...

WHO ARE YOU?

ER... B-BOND, JAMES BOND...

BOND! I THOUGHT I RECOGNIZED YOU...

LIFE ON THE OPEN ROAD, EH, JIMMY-BOY?

DON'T GET COCKY.

HELLEBORE WILL HAVE PHONED AHEAD.

WE'VE STILL GOT TO CONVINCE THE POLICE. WHO DO YOU THINK THEY'RE MORE LIKELY TO BELIEVE?

WE'RE JUST KIDS STEALING A LORRY.

HELL. THEY'RE ALREADY ON TO US.

THEY DON'T KNOW ABOUT ME.

YOU COULD GET HELP WHILE THEY CHASE AFTER ME.

WE'LL HAVE TO FIND SOMEWHERE TO HIDE YOU.

WE CAN'T GO BACK TO KEITHLY...NOT YET.

WHY ON EARTH NOT?

HELLEBORE'S DOING THINGS ...AWFUL THINGS.

AND YOU THINK YOU CAN STOP HIM?

I HAVE TO TRY...

...BECAUSE THERE'S NO ONE ELSE WHO CAN.

ALL RIGHT THEN. LET'S GO.

YOU'RE IN LUCK. THERE'S A MIST ON THE LOCH.

IT'LL HIDE OUR APPROACH.

BUT YOU'VE STILL GOT TO GET PAST THE GUARDS.

ARE YOU ALWAYS THIS PESSIMISTIC?

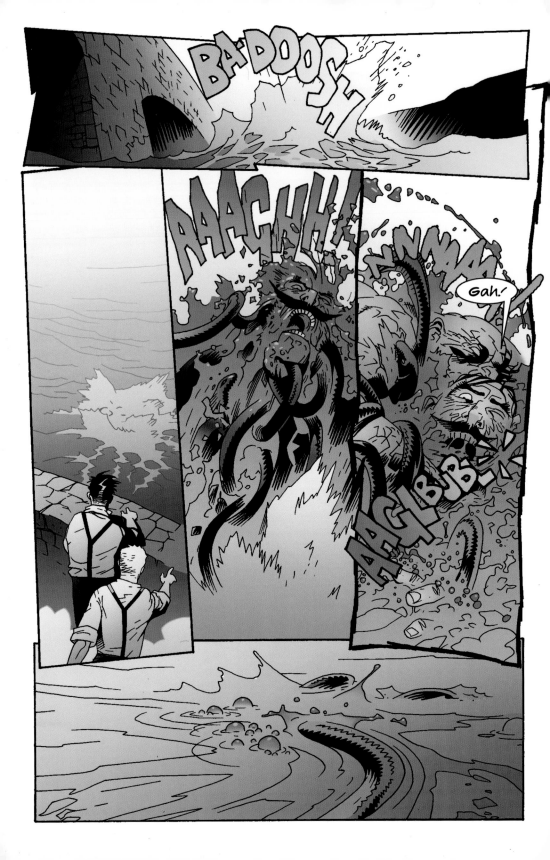

"THEY CAME FOR ME IN THE NIGHT.

"THEY DIDN'T TREAT ME VERY WELL."

"YOU ESCAPED OBVIOUSLY..."

"NOBODY CAN HOLD A BOND FOREVER...EH?

"JAMES, IF YOU'LL TAKE SOME ADVICE FROM ME...

"DON'T EVER BE A SPY..."

Adapted from the novel *SilverFin: A James Bond Adventure* by Charlie Higson
Adapted by Kev Walker
Scripted by Charlie Higson and Kev Walker
Lettering by Annie Parkhouse

Published by Disney · Hyperion Books, an imprint of Disney Book Group. No part of this book may be reproduced or transmitted in any form or by any means, electronic or mechanical, including photocopying, recording, or by any information storage and retrieval system, without written permission from the publisher.

For information address Disney · Hyperion Books,
114 Fifth Avenue, New York, New York 10011-5690.

First American edition, 2010
10 9 8 7 6 5 4 3 2 1
Printed in Singapore

Library of Congress Cataloging-in-Publication Data on file.
ISBN 978-1-4231-3022-2 (hardcover)
ISBN 978-1-4231-3023-9 (paperback)

Visit www.youngbond.com and www.hyperionbooksforchildren.com